The author is grateful to the following expert readers and advisors:
Jeanne Cannella Schmitzer, assistant director, Falling Water River Regional Library,
and adjunct professor of history, Tennessee Tech University
Donald C. Boyd, chief of historical research and senior historian, U.S. Air Force, AFRC
Neil Kasiak, oral historian, Appalachian Equine Project, Eastern Kentucky University
Helen Wykle, archivist and historian, Pine Mountain Settlement School
Rich Haynes, director, Harlan County Public Library

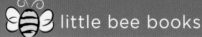 little bee books

New York, NY
Text copyright © 2021 by Emma Carlson Berne
Illustrations copyright © 2021 by Ilaria Urbinati
Manufactured in China RRD 1220
littlebeebooks.com
First Edition
2 4 6 8 10 9 7 5 3 1

For information about special discounts on bulk purchases,
please contact Little Bee Books at sales@littlebeebooks.com.

ISBN 978-1-4998-1173-5

miles long, and they crossed creeks with names like Greasy Creek, Troublesome, and Cut Shin. Often, they rode right in the creek beds—that was the easiest way to reach some of the cabins.

Riding through moving creeks was dangerous. Sometimes, the water came all the way up to their horses' chests. In the winter, the animals' hooves punched through thin ice to the black water beneath. Librarians' feet were often frozen to the stirrups.

But people wanted those books. Especially books with pictures. Even if they could not read, they could look. They wanted stories about other corners of the world. Reading about faraway places like Kenya or even California was like opening up the mountains a little, to let the outside world in.

Often, people were uncomfortable taking free library books without giving something back. So, when the packhorse librarians would hand out books, women would give them recipes or quilt patterns in return.

The librarians pasted those recipes and patterns into binders to make their own books. These books were carried on their routes to be loaned out at various stops. Because of this, women could share their recipes and patterns with each other.

Packhorse librarians rode thousands of miles and brought books to people for nine years before the program ended. Because of them, people saw that traveling libraries could work. In the 1950s, more roads were built in the mountains, and Kentucky and many other states started bringing books to people by truck and car. Today, librarians drive "bookmobiles" up to farms and cabins in the mountains. The packhorse librarians are gone. But the libraries they carried in their saddlebags are not.

BIBLIOGRAPHY

Appalachian Equine Project, William H. Berge Oral History Center, Eastern Kentucky University.

Boyd, Donald C. Phone interview. March 11, 2019.

——. "The Book Women of Kentucky: The WPA Pack Horse Library Project, 1936-1943." *Libraries & the Cultural Record*, Vol. 42, No. 2, 2007.

——. "The WPA Pack Horse Library Program and the Social Utility of Literacy, 1883-1962." Dissertation, University of Florida, 2009.

Haynes, Rich. Phone interview. February 28, 2019.

Goodman-Paxton Photographic Collection, University of Kentucky.

Kasiak, Neil. Phone interview. February 26, 2019.

Pine Mountain Settlement School Collection, https://pinemountainsettlement.net/

"Ruth Shuler Dieter." *Pine Mountain Settlement School Collections.* https://pinemountainsettlement.net/?page_id=3185

Schmitzer, Jeanne Cannella. Phone interview. March 4, 2019.

——. "The Pack-Horse Library Project of Eastern Kentucky: 1936-1943." Master's thesis, University of Tennessee, 1998.

Various recorded interviews. William H. Berge Oral History Center, Eastern Kentucky University.

Wykle, Helen, Preston Jones, and Ann Angell Bissell. Phone interview. February 27, 2019.

AUTHOR'S NOTE

When I set out to write this book, I thought of myself as a child, packed into the back of an orange Toyota Camry next to my brother, traveling from our home in Cincinnati, Ohio, across Kentucky, to Huntington, West Virginia. There, we would visit my great-grandmother, Alva Hutchinson.

Alva was born in the Appalachian Mountains in 1902. She left school in the sixth grade, still mostly illiterate. Later in her life, she taught herself to read.

The mountains around my great-grandmother's home were green, rumpled, and dripping. In the narrow hollers, towering slabs of rock cut off the sky. Down there, houses were arranged in lines beside powerful, churning rivers. I went to this place in my mind when I set out to tell the story of a packhorse librarian. I thought of Alva in her cat's-eye glasses on the couch in her little house. This story is for her.

❀ ❀ ❀

In eastern Kentucky in the 1930s, many people lived deep within the Appalachian Mountains. The hillsides were steep with deep and narrow valleys. People called these mountain valleys "hollers."

In the hollers, people built log cabins perched on rocks they pried by hand out of hillsides. Their horses helped them plow small gardens and fields. Their cabins were far apart, and towns were very far away. In many places, there were no roads at all as the mountains proved too steep and rocky.

But the people who lived in hollers knew how to get around. They walked through creek beds to get to each other's homes. They built swinging bridges across the creeks and bred their own special horses that were good at going up and down hills without falling.

But without roads, the outside world stayed out. And people stayed in. Books stayed out, too.

Many of these people had never heard of libraries. Most didn't have books or magazines in their houses. Some adults could read, but many more couldn't. Often, schoolhouses had few books or none at all. Kentucky's librarians thought this was wrong. Children and grown-ups who lived in the mountains should have library books just like everyone else, they said. The U.S. government agreed.

During this time, many people in the country had lost their jobs and their money. This time was called the Great Depression. The people in the mountains had also suffered greatly. Many people worked in coal mines, some of which had closed. People who were already poor became poorer.

President Franklin Roosevelt created programs to help people find work. The Works Progress Administration (WPA) was one of these. The WPA offered to fund the salaries for librarians in eastern Kentucky who, in turn, would make jobs by creating traveling libraries.

Horses were the only way librarians could get books to people. Trucks and wagons were no good on the steep slopes. But the special mountain horses were.

Local teenagers and young women were hired. They'd ridden horses in the hollers since they were tiny children. And these new librarians weren't afraid of long hours in the saddle or any snow or rain.

The librarians carried their books in whatever they could find—grain sacks, pillowcases, or saddlebags. At every house and school, they would drop books off and pick books up. Their routes were about eighteen

"The children are waiting, Dan," Edith says. "Let's go!"

William and Ruth crowd against Edith's knees as she tells
the story of a magic sword buried in a stone. Even Mr. Caudill listens.
By the time she's finished, the storm has passed.

Edith still has more families to visit.
The creeks are going to be extra dangerous after the rain.
Mounted again, Edith waves goodbye.

"Did you bring me an adventure story?" William asks.

"Of course, I did!" Edith hands down the book sack so they can choose.

"And I have a pawpaw pudding recipe for you, Mrs. Caudill."

Outside, the rain beats against the cabin walls,
but inside, Edith pulls a chair close to the woodstove.
Mrs. Caudill hands her a mug of coffee.
She opens the storybook and starts to read.

Crash! A tree smashes down, right in front of them.
No time to stop!
Edith and Dan clear it in one spectacular leap.

"The book woman's here! The book woman's here!" William shouts.
He and his sister Ruth are waiting on the cabin porch.
"I knew she wouldn't forget!"

Edith and Dan trot into the yard, breathing hard.
Mr. Caudill hurries to open the barn door for Dan.

A flash of lightning slashes across the sky.
Dan jumps as thunder booms, echoing through the hills.
"Easy, boy!" she says. She pats his neck as the rain starts.

The wind rises to a scream, bending the treetops.
Edith pulls on her coat as rain drips off the brim of her hat and pelts Dan's rump.
"Come on, Dan!" Edith shouts.
She slaps his shoulder with the reins. Dan springs into a gallop.

Edith pulls out her lunch.
Two biscuits and some ham.
Dan snuffles at the fresh grass.

The rumpled mountains spread out below them.
Edith can just see the Caudills' cabin, nestled in a holler three miles away.

Partway down the other side of Piney Knob,
a little spring bubbles.

Edith is thirsty.
She drinks and splashes the cool,
limestone water against her hot face.

Edith lashes the book sack to the saddle. She slides down and hugs Dan's damp neck.

Edith leads Dan up the ridge. Thorny branches slap at her face.

Rocks slide under her feet, tumbling down to Troublesome Creek. "We're almost there, Dan!"

At the top, Edith and Dan rest and breathe.
The sun peeks out from behind the storm clouds and warms their faces.

Dan surges forward, straining, climbing
toward the top of the ridge high above them.
He snorts and blows. His ribs heave.
"You can do it, Dan!" Edith says.

But Dan has to stop.
Piney Knob is too steep,
and Edith is too heavy.

Water splashes up onto Dan's chest. Edith grips the book sack tight. If her books get wet, they'll be ruined.

Past the creek, Piney Knob Ridge
thrusts its shoulders into the sky.
But Edith is not afraid.
She's climbed these slopes since she was a little girl.

"Looks like a storm is coming, Dan," Edith says.
Dan nickers as she hoists his saddle.
"We better hurry."

Dan picks his way down the steep slope to Troublesome Creek.
Edith and Dan slide and slip, scrabbling in the slick mud.

Edith is a packhorse librarian.
Every day, she travels for miles to deliver books.
William lives far back in the mountains.
Edith will have to ride hard to reach his family's cabin.

Edith laces her boots and slaps on her hat.
As she stuffs storybooks, magazines, and her lunch into her book sack,
she hears the distant crack of thunder.

Books by Horseback

A Librarian's Brave Journey to Deliver Books to Children

words by EMMA CARLSON BERNE   *pictures by* ILARIA URBINATI

little bee books

The Kentucky dawn is gray and chilly.
But Edith is already awake and pasting a torn book.
She promised eight-year-old William Caudill
that she would bring him an adventure story today.